# Kingdom Quest:

## Will You Follow the Prince?

### A Faith-Filled Adventure Where Every Choice Matters

By
Heather Lyn Davis

Copyright © 2023 by Heather Davis | Published by Heather's Helpful Stories.

Author of:
*I Can Sleep When the Wind Blows*
*Meet Jane and Bobby*
*The Blomes & the Smooms and the Impossible Bridge*
*Into Justin's World*
*Jake the Ape Makes a Lot of Mistakes*
*Freddy the Fox Will Not Share His Thoughts*

All rights reserved.

No portion of this book may be reproduced or used in any manner whatsoever without the express written permission of the publisher except for the use of brief quotations in a book review.

Printed in China.

Written by Heather Lyn Davis
Illustrated by Corryn Webb

ISBN: 979-8-9866225-6-9

Edited by Brooke Vitale
Designed and formatted by Ryan Webb

For permission requests, contact
Heather Lyn Davis - Best Selling Children's Book Author
Phone Number: 208-994-3527
Email: Heathershelpfulstories@gmail.com
Website: www.heathershelpfulstories.com

"Inspiring, engaging stories that teach lessons about diversity, self-confidence, working together, inclusion and growth mindset."

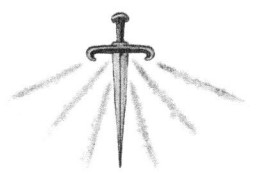

# Chapter 1: The Two Princes

There once was a mighty and merciful King who ruled with wisdom and love. His kingdom stretched across green valleys, sparkling rivers, and sunlit cities. But beyond the mountains lay a shadowed land, where the light of the King's presence didn't reach.

The King had two sons. The younger son was clever, but proud. His eyes gleamed with ambition. He dreamed of ruling the kingdom in his own way—without waiting, without sharing.

The older son was joyful and gentle. He loved the King, and he loved the people. His heart delighted in kindness, and his joy came from serving others.

But one day, the younger son grew restless. He didn't want to wait. He wanted the throne now. And he didn't want to share it.

So, he began to whisper to others. He said the King's way was too slow, too hard. He promised a faster path. An easier way.

Whispers turned to arguments. Arguments turned

to rebellion. Before long, a war began. The kingdom was torn in two. The older prince stood by the King, his armor shining like dawn. But the younger prince led his followers into battle, storming the borders of peace.

*Now you must choose:*

*If you stand with the good prince and the King,* turn to Chapter 2 (page 4).

*If you're not sure and want to hear what the younger prince has to say,*
turn to Chapter 3 (page 6).

# Chapter 2: Loyal to the King

You stand beside the good prince. You trust the King's wisdom, even if it's hard. You know love must be chosen, not forced.

The war rages across hills and skies. Thunder claps. Swords clash. But in the end, the good prince and the King are victorious. The younger prince is cast out to the farthest edge of the land—where light fades and bitterness grows.

But peace doesn't last long...

*Turn to Chapter 4 (page 8).*

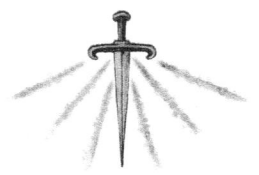

# Chapter 3: The Tempting Voice

The younger prince's voice is strong. He talks of greatness. Of ruling with strength. Of a kingdom where everyone always does the right thing—because they have no choice.

At first, it sounds good. Safe. Easy.

But something in your heart doesn't feel right. The sky above him is gray. His words feel heavy.

Then you hear the good prince. His words are quiet, but full of light.

"There is still time to choose," he says.

You step away from the shadows.

*Turn to Chapter 2 (page 4).*

# Chapter 4: The Hidden Prison

The exiled prince is furious. In the shadowlands, he builds traps and snares. Thorny paths wind into dark woods. At the center of his twisted land, he creates a prison. Cold. Cracked. Inescapable.

He sends whispers into the kingdom: Come see what you're missing. Come play. It's harmless. Just a little closer.

Many are caught. They disappear beyond the border.

The King is heartbroken. He watches from the high tower. He longs to bring His people home. He calls for a volunteer to go into the prison and lead them out.

The good prince steps forward. "I will go."

Now the journey begins.

**Turn to Chapter 5 (page 10).**

# Chapter 5: The Prince Warns the People

The good prince walks toward the border. His cloak brushes the dust. His lantern glows with steady light. Along the way, he stops to warn the people.

"There are traps ahead. The prison is real. If you get caught, you cannot escape on your own. Please be careful. Stay far from the snares in the shadowlands."

Some people listen. Others laugh at him. Some turn their backs. The air near the border grows colder.

*Now you must choose:*

*If you stop and listen to the prince's warning, turn to Chapter 6 (page 12).*

*If you go with your friends just to see for yourself—you're sure you won't get too close—turn to Chapter 7 (page 14).*

*If you believe you're strong and smart enough to handle the traps,* turn to Chapter 8 (page 16).

*If you walk away, unsure what you should do,* turn to Chapter 9 (page 18).

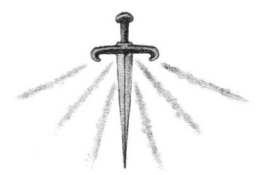

# Chapter 6: You Follow the Prince

You slow your steps. The crowd thins. The wind softens.

Something in the prince's voice wraps around your heart—like warmth, and peace, and home.

"I believe you," you say quietly. "But . . . what if I've already come too close?"

The prince turns to you. His eyes shine like morning sun through mist. "Then stay close to me," he says. "And I will help you find the way back."

You nod. You take a deep breath and walk with him.

*Turn to Chapter 10 (page 20).*

# Chapter 7: You Go With Your Friends

"It's just a little walk," one of your friends says. Laughter dances on the breeze. "We're not going to do anything bad."

You nod. The air near the border is cool, sharp. "We're smart. We'll be careful."

But the ground beneath your feet shifts. The light grows dim. The path is slippery, and the traps are easy to miss.

One minute you're walking. The next—you're falling.

The prison is darker than you imagined. The air is heavy, and your voice echoes off the cold stone. You don't know how to get out.

*Turn to Chapter 13 (page 26).*

# Chapter 8: You Rely on Your Own Strength

"I can take care of myself," you say. You lift your chin. "No trap is going to catch me."

You step boldly. You watch your feet. But you didn't see the snare—it was hidden beneath soft grass and glowing moss.

You cry out, but the trees stand silent. Cold walls rise up around you, sealing out the sky.

You are in the prison now.

But just when you feel most alone, a whisper brushes your heart like wind through a crack in the stone: "I came for you."

*Turn to Chapter 13 (page 26).*

# Chapter 9: You Walk Away to Think

You don't want to admit it... but something the prince said won't leave you alone.

You find a quiet place where the grass bends gently and the border disappears into mist. You sit. You listen.

You think about the traps. About the people you've seen disappear. About the prince's promise.

You aren't sure yet what to do. But you're listening now.

And the next time he passes by, you'll be ready to follow.

*Turn to Chapter 6 (page 12).*

# Chapter 10:
# You Walk With the Prince

The prince smiles when you walk beside him. His steps are steady. His voice is calm and clear.

He stops to warn others, just like he warned you. Some listen and nod. Others scoff and roll their eyes. Some don't even notice him at all.

You wish they could feel what you feel—that quiet, safe light that seems to glow just from being near him.

Then you see it: the border. The line where safety ends and shadow begins. The wind shifts. The ground changes.

"Stay close," he says. "I may be taken, but don't be afraid. I promised I would come for you."

*Turn to Chapter 11 (page 22).*

# Chapter 11: The Capture

It happens fast—like a storm breaking through the stillness.

Guards leap from behind twisted trees. Their armor is jagged. Their voices are sharp.

You try to stop them—but the prince gently holds up a hand.

"It has to be this way," he says, his voice like calm in the chaos. "I must go into the prison so I can open the way for others."

They beat him. They laugh at him. And they drag him into the darkness.

"No!" you cry out.

But he turns back one last time. His eyes meet yours. "Remember what I told you. I will lead them out."

And then he is gone.

The forest is silent again. But not your heart.

You step forward ... into the shadows.

### Turn to Chapter 13 (page 26).

## Chapter 12: While You Wait

The Prince is gone—for now. And still . . . you remember.

You sit in the dim silence of your cell. The stone beneath you is cold, but your heart carries a warmth that wasn't there before. Not since you heard his voice. Not since you saw the light in his eyes and felt, even for a moment, what it means to be free.

You're waiting now. Not with fear—but with faith.

And as you wait, you whisper. You speak softly to the others. To the weary. To the wounded. To those who've stopped hoping.

You tell them about the Prince— about how he knew your name. How he touched your chains. How he called you beloved.

Some don't believe you. But some . . . lean in.

And though you do not walk beside him yet, your heart is walking toward him.

He will come again. He always comes again.

And when you hear his voice once more— maybe you'll rise. Maybe you'll run. Maybe you'll lead others to the door.

Because the story isn't over. Not for you. Not for anyone.

The Prince is not finished. And neither are you.

# Chapter 13: Inside the Prison

The prison is cold. And dark. It feels hopeless. But the prince is here. And he is calling.

"Follow me," he says. "I know the way out. I will set you free."

His voice is steady and sure. But the way he points to? It's narrow. Rocky. Shadowy. His way will not be easy. You can only see by the light he carries.

Others begin to follow. Some stumble. Some cry out. Some fall behind.

And now it's your turn to choose:

*If you follow him in trust and faith, turn to Chapter 14 (page 28).*

*If you wait to see if others are safe first before you try to follow, turn to Chapter 15 (page 30).*

*If you try to find your own way out, turn to Chapter 16 (page 32).*

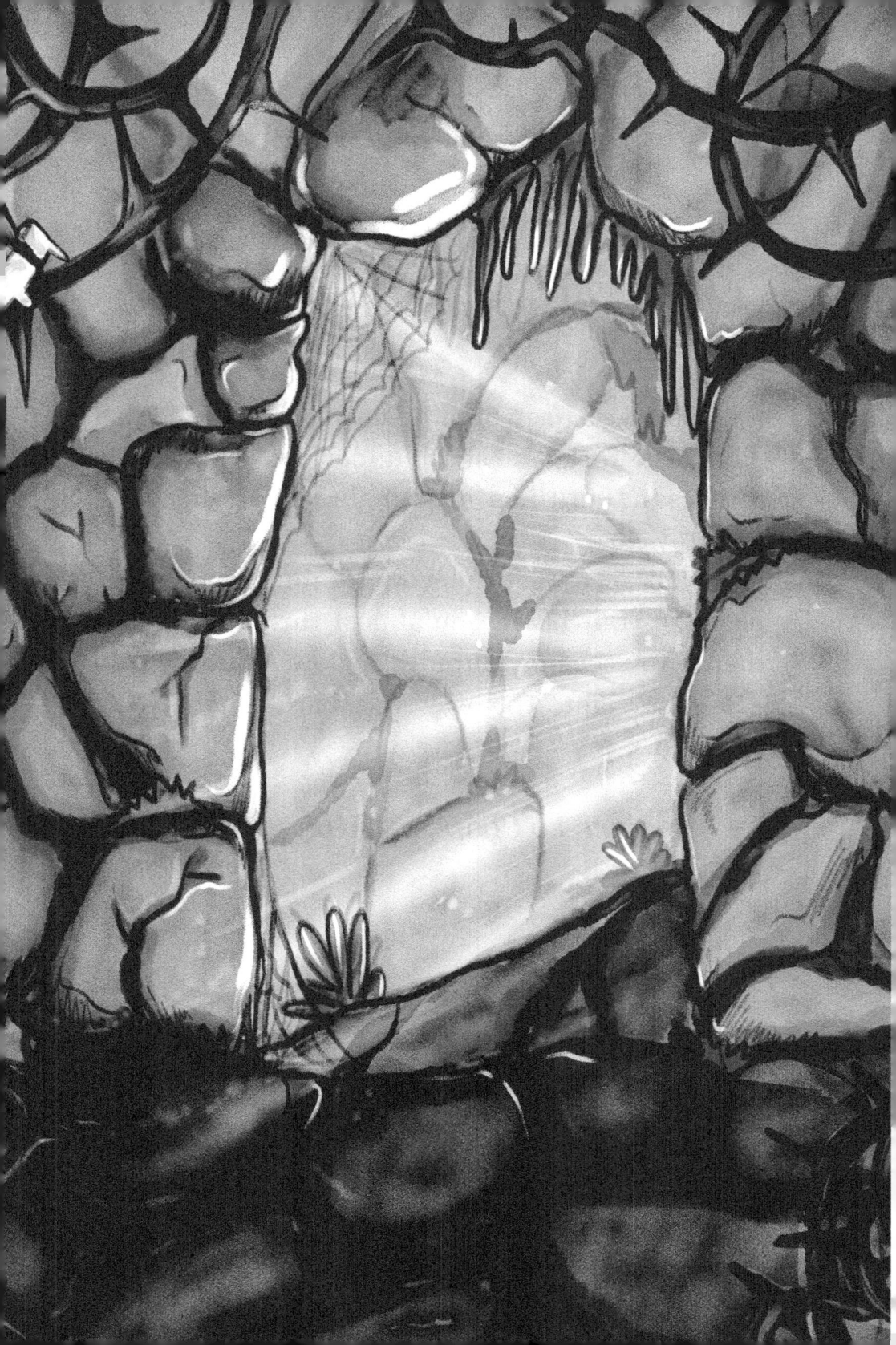

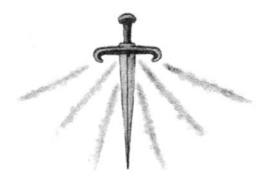

# Chapter 14: The Hard Path

You take a deep breath—and a step.

The rocks are sharp underfoot. The darkness presses in. But the prince's light shines ahead. And you stay close.

You fall once. He helps you up. You cry. He speaks peace to your heart. You almost turn back . . . but then— You see it: A glimmer. A glow. A door of light.

He was right. The way was hard, but it led to freedom.

*Turn to Chapter 17 (page 34).*

# Chapter 15: You Stay Behind

You watch as the others follow the prince. Their path is steep and difficult. You hear a stumble. A sob.

Your heart tightens. You want to believe. But you're afraid.

"It's safer here," you whisper. "It's not good . . . but it's familiar."

And yet—when you close your eyes, you still hear his voice: "I'm coming again. I will not give up on you."

And deep down, you know the way is still open.

And then . . . you see a flicker.

The prince is there. Holding out his hand.

"Are you ready now?" he asks.

You are.

*Turn to Chapter 18.*

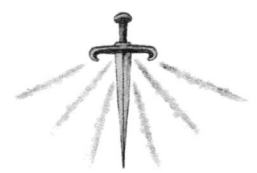

# Chapter 16: You Try to Escape Alone

"I've been here a long time," you say. "I know these halls. I can do it myself."

You walk. Left. Right. Turn. Again. Again.

The tunnels twist. The walls close in. There's no light—and no exit.

You sit down, tired and lost. And still, you start to feel hope that the prince will come back for you.

**Turn to Chapter 18.**

## Chapter 17: Freedom and Welcome

You step into the light. The air is warm. The sun touches your face.

And the King is running to you.

"My child," He says, gathering you in His arms. "You are home. You are safe. My son brought you back to me."

You look beside you. The prince is there. Smiling. Glowing. Scarred... but filled with joy.

You made it. But your heart still aches—because you remember the others. Still trapped. Still hurting.

*Turn to Chapter 19.*

# Chapter 18: Hope Remains

You didn't follow him. Not today. But the memory of his voice lives in your heart.

When you hear it again, maybe you'll rise. Maybe you'll run to him.

Because the door has not closed.

And the prince—never stops coming for his people.

*Turn to Chapter 12 (page 24).*

# Chapter 19: Becoming a Light

The prince turns to you. His eyes are kind. "There are still others," he says. "Still trapped. Still afraid. Will you help me find them?"

You nod.

"They don't all know me yet," he says. "But they might follow you, if you shine your light."

He hands you a lantern.

It's small—but enough to light the path.

You step back toward the tunnels. Not as a prisoner. But as a rescuer.

And you whisper, just like he did: "Follow me. I know the way out."

**The End (and the beginning).**

# Your Story Matters

## *Discussion Questions + Journal Pages*

Use these pages to reflect on your own journey and the choices you make each day. You can talk with your family, write your thoughts, or draw what you feel.

_____
_____
_____
_____
_____
_____
_____
_____
_____
_____
_____
_____
_____
_____
_____
_____
_____
_____
_____
_____

# Everyday Choices

What are some choices you make every day that show who you want to follow?

### My thoughts:
_____
_____
_____
_____
_____
_____
_____

Have you ever been tempted to do something you knew wasn't right? What helped you choose a better way?

### My thoughts:
_____
_____
_____
_____
_____

Are there times when doing the right thing feels hard? What helps you keep going?

## *My thoughts:*

_____
_____
_____
_____
_____
_____
_____
_____
_____
_____
_____
_____
_____
_____
_____
_____
_____
_____
_____
_____
_____
_____
_____
_____
_____

# Listening for Warnings

Who in your life helps you know what's safe and what's dangerous? How are they like the good prince in the story?

*My thoughts:*
_____
_____
_____
_____
_____
_____

What are some commandments or teachings from Jesus that help you stay safe?

*My thoughts:*
_____
_____
_____
_____
_____
_____

# Getting Close to the Traps

What are some things in life that might seem fun at first—but could pull us away from what's right?

### *My thoughts:*

_____
_____
_____
_____
_____
_____
_____

How can you notice when you're getting too close to something that could hurt you?

### *My thoughts:*

_____
_____
_____
_____
_____
_____
_____

# Jesus Will Always Come for You

Why do you think Jesus chose to suffer to save us—even when we don't always listen?

## My thoughts:

_____
_____
_____
_____
_____
_____
_____
_____
_____
_____
_____
_____
_____
_____
_____
_____
_____
_____
_____
_____
_____
_____

What does it mean to follow Him, even when the path is hard?

## My thoughts:

_____
_____
_____
_____
_____
_____
_____
_____
_____
_____
_____
_____
_____
_____
_____
_____
_____
_____
_____
_____

# Becoming a Light

How can you be like the prince in someone else's life?

## My thoughts:
_____
_____
_____
_____
_____
_____
_____

What does it look like to shine your light at school, in your family, or at church?

## My thoughts:
_____
_____
_____
_____
_____
_____
_____

# One Final Question

If you were one of the people in this story... Which path would you choose today—and why?

## *My thoughts:*

_____
_____
_____
_____
_____
_____
_____
_____
_____
_____
_____
_____
_____
_____
_____
_____
_____
_____
_____
_____

# My Notes

Made in the USA
Coppell, TX
19 September 2025